Margaret Leroy

ARISTOTLE SLUDGE

A MODERN-DAY DINOSAUR

"Just look at him!"

"Ah, isn't he sweet!"

"What IS he, miss?"

"Ugh, he's all wrinkled."

"Babies ARE wrinkled," said Tracy who had eight brothers and sisters and knew about these things.

"Yuk, he's all sludgey."

"Look at his funny arms . . . like – like great big elbows."

"What IS he, miss? What is he, d'you think?"

Margaret Leroy

ARISTOTLE SLUDGE
A MODERN-DAY DINOSAUR

Illustrated by Natalie Bould

Hippo Books
Scholastic Publications Limited
London

Scholastic Publications Ltd,
10 Earlham Street, London WC2H 9RX, UK

Scholastic Inc.,
730 Broadway, New York, NY 10003, USA

Scholastic Canada Ltd,
123 Newkirk Road, Richmond Hill,
Ontario L4C 3G5, Canada

Ashton Scholastic Pty Ltd,
PO Box 579, Gosford, New South Wales,
Australia

Ashton Scholastic Ltd,
165 Marua Road, Panmure, Auckland 6,
New Zealand

Published by Scholastic Publications Ltd, 1990

Text Copyright © Margaret Leroy 1991
Illustrations copyright © Natalie Bould, 1991

ISBN 0 590 76414 4

Made and printed by Cox & Wyman Ltd, Reading, Berks
Typeset by Goodfellow & Egan, Cambridge

Chapter One

The Hatching

"How can we draw a dinosaur, when we've never even seen one?" said Tracy crossly.

"What d'you mean, never?" said Rakesh. "Here's Jason sitting right beside you, and you say you've never seen a dinosaur!"

Jason said nothing – he wasn't good with words. But his leg moved very quickly under the table. Rakesh yelped and clutched his ankle. But he couldn't kick back, for the Purgle's eye was on him. Miss Purgletwitch could be difficult when she was cross. He moved his chair a little to one side and settled down to his drawing.

"I wonder what they were really like," said Tania thoughtfully. "That bird with teeth, for one . . . that ptero-what's it."

"Pterosaurus, silly." John was the Class 1C expert on dinosaurs. "An order of toothed birds, rather like lizards with wings. Now extinct."

"I'm glad they died out," said Dawn. "I bet they were ever so fierce."

"Oh, flying fishsticks," said Tracy. "I'm sick of the stupid thing."

John leaned over her drawing.
He chuckled to himself. "Hey, take a
look at this, folks! Well, well, well!
Whoever saw a jam pudding with
wings?"

Jason laughed loudly. He always
laughed at John's jokes. John smiled
a little to himself.

Tracy threw down her pen in disgust. "Oh, I give up," she said. "I'm going to make a model." And she went to the stock-cupboard in search of yoghurt cartons.

The cupboard was in rather a mess that day. Someone had spilt some material scraps all over the floor. There were pieces of velvet and bits of Christmas tinsel, all mixed up with newspaper and egg-boxes. Tracy decided to do some tidying up. She was class monitor in charge of the stock-cupboard. And she knew Mr Tompsett would be pleased. Mr Tompsett was the caretaker, and a special friend of Tracy's, and it was said that messy cupboards made smoke come out of his ears.

Tracy shut the door of the cupboard behind her. She heard a fight break out in the classroom. Jason was thumping somebody. Miss Purgletwitch was shouting at him. There was a shrill edge to her voice, like there often was on rainy days or just before Christmas, or any time things were specially lively. Tracy smiled to herself. It all sounded very far away . . . like being in a cave by the sea, where you hear the waves break outside but know they can't touch you.

Tracy didn't turn on the light. She set to work by the thin gleam that came from under the door. She piled the newspaper into a big fat pile, and stuffed all the fabric tidily back in the bag. It was a solemn

5

secret feeling, working away in the dark.

There were some new things in the cupboard that day. The Headmaster was always complaining that he didn't have enough money for books and paints and paper. Sometimes people would ring and say they had things to give to the school, and Mr Tompsett would go off and collect them. He must have been collecting recently: there were some paint-boxes and books and magazines that she hadn't seen before, piled up at the back of the cupboard next to the yoghurt cartons. The books had faded leather covers with the titles in spidery gilt lettering. They looked very old. And in a flowerpot were some quill pens, like people used for writing a long time ago. Tracy wondered where he'd got them from. Some weird old house perhaps. She poked around to see what else there was.

It was in a giant pineapple yoghurt carton that she found it. Her fingers closed over something cool and smooth and quite unexpected. She held it up in the gleam of light from

the door. "Flying fishsticks!" said Tracy. It was an egg, a large pale egg. Not at all the sort of thing you expect to find in a stock-cupboard. Pale, watery colours gleamed on its surface, like streaks of paint that had run together. Blue and green like jungles, and soft sludge brown.

Tracy stood quite still and looked at the egg for a moment. The noise from the classroom washed against the cupboard door. She opened the door a little. It was a good moment. Miss Purgletwitch was busy with Jason in the Quiet Room, the little reading room that opened off from the classroom behind her desk. She seemed to be trying to sort out who'd started the fight. Tracy slipped out of the cupboard, the egg firmly grasped in her hand, and went to sit next to Dawn.

"Look!" she hissed.

"What on earth . . .?"

"Found it in a yoghurt carton."

"Wow!" Dawn touched it carefully with one finger. "Look at all those colours."

"And just what are you two up to?"

A shadow fell across the table. Tracy looked up to meet Miss Purgletwitch's glare. She looked cross and slightly scared, and her earrings glittered as they waggled angrily.

Tracy decided on the direct approach. She held the egg up in her hand.

"Found it in a yoghurt carton."

The Purgle stared at the egg in a

worried way. Perhaps she thought it was some sort of joke, that might explode if she touched it.

"Well, you'd better . . . er . . . take it to the Nature Table."

So Tracy put the egg on the Nature Table, between the shrivelled seaweed and Dawn's buttercups. And she and Dawn moved their chairs up close to the table, to keep an eye on things.

"Cor, that's a big 'un," said Jason. He picked it up. "Cor, it's quite a weight."

"Leave it alone," said Tracy fiercely.

"It's nice," said Tania, coming up. "Like those pink marble eggs you get in gift shops."

"That's a GINORMOUS egg,"

10

said John. "Didn't know you had it in you!" Jason, who always laughed at John's jokes, nearly fell off his chair.

"Where d'you find it, Trace?" said Rakesh.

"In the stock-cupboard."

"You what? Come off it, Tracy!"

Tracy bit her lip. "I told you, I found it in the stock-cupboard."

"Very funny!" said John nastily. "Very funny indeed. Ha, ha!"

"What lives in a cupboard and lays eggs?" crowed Rakesh. "All together now . . . T.R.A.C.Y. TRACY!"

Tracy bit her lip again, and tried to shut her ears to the chant. But the others went on laughing, and What-Lives-In-A-Cupboard-And-Lays-Eggs became the Class 1C joke for the whole morning.

11

It wasn't till halfway through Sums that they all stopped laughing. The Purgle was on abacus placings at the time.

" . . . And then you move your ten hundreds to this column and . . . Rakesh will you stop making that stupid noise?"

"It's not me miss," said Rakesh, looking hurt. His ruler for once was lying quietly on his desk.

" . . . And so we have two thousands in this column and . . . John, is it you?"

"ME, miss?" said John.

They could all hear it now, a steady tapping sound.

"Who is it then?" said Miss Purgletwitch, looking round the class desperately. "If someone doesn't own up soon, I'm keeping the lot of you in after school."

But no hands were raised. Everyone sat and listened as the noise increased. The tapping grew until it was like drumbeats, signalling for battle to begin.

"I shall get the Headmaster," wailed Miss Purgletwitch above the furious drumming. Dawn stuffed her fingers in her ears.

"Please miss," shouted Tracy, "it's the egg!"

The drumming became a hammering that echoed round the walls of the classroom. The hammering grew faster and louder, like a power drill. Then came the explosion, with a bang that made the walls of the classroom shake and the books dance on the shelves.

The shrivelled seaweed and Dawn's buttercups fell off the Nature Table. Dawn and Tracy were pelted with hard bits of something. Lumps of sticky jelly, like gooseberry jam, spattered down from the ceiling. A strong sour smell hung in the air.

Miss Purgletwitch poked her head out from under her desk. "Revolting!" she gasped, holding her nose.

Then in the silence came a new sound, a soggy sodden grizzling whimpering sound. Everyone turned to the Nature Table.

"Please miss," said Tracy, pulling sticky bits of shell out of her hair. "Please miss, it's the egg! It's hatched!"

Chapter Two

In Mr Tompsett's Den

Felt-tips and folders went flying as
Class 1C stampeded to the Nature
Table. Poor Miss Purgletwitch could
hardly keep her footing.

"Flying fishsticks, isn't he funny!"

The Nature Table rocked
dangerously as the tidal wave of
children broke against it. The
shrivelled seaweed and Dawn's
buttercups were trodden underfoot.

15

"Just look at him!"

"Ah, isn't he sweet!"

"What IS he, miss?"

"Ugh, he's all wrinkled."

"Babies ARE wrinkled," said Tania, who had eight brothers and sisters and knew about these things.

"Yuk, he's all sludgey."

"Look at his funny arms . . . like – like great big elbows."

"What IS he, miss? What is he, d'you think?"

"Perhaps we'd better . . . er . . . clear up the mess," said Miss Purgletwitch, not very hopefully. But nobody moved. They all just stood there, staring at the whimpering baby-thing. He looked back at them with deep dark eyes and his long beak gleamed with

16

newness. Then he started to shuffle
round the Nature Table, wobbling a
bit as he tried to get used to his legs.

"Ah, look at him, poor little birdie!"

"Birds don't have four legs," said
John indignantly. "I'd say he's more
like a lizard."

17

"Hey, look at his eyes – they're green!"

"He's all skin and bone, poor little thing!"

"Look, he's shivering – he must be cold!"

"What should we do with him, miss?"

"Perhaps we'd better . . . er . . . put him in a box," said Miss Purgletwitch, looking longingly at her watch.

Tracy remembered a big carton in the stock-cupboard. She brought it out, stuffed with crumpled newspaper.

"He's all soft and squashy," she said, picking him up with gentle fingers and tucking him up in the newspaper nest.

18

"But what IS he, miss?"

Miss Purgletwitch made a kind of desperate grunt. "Yes, well, that's a very interesting question. But if you think I'm going to find all the answers for you . . ."

Just then the bell went for lunch. Miss Purgletwitch turned and fled for the safety of the staffroom.

Class 1C was on First Lunch that day. And most of the class rushed off in search of chips and chocolate pudding. But Tracy's friends stood guard by the cardboard box. As Dawn said, "He's Ours, and we can't leave him alone."

"Not with Class 1D on the warpath," added Rakesh.

Tania peered in the carton. "Ah

look, he's fast asleep," she said, peering fondly at the soggy shape that had curled up cosily in the crumpled newspaper.

"When he wakes up he'll be hungry," said Tracy, who knew about babies.

"But how shall we know what to feed him on," said John, "when we don't know what he is?"

There was silence. Everyone stared at John.

"It's a problem," said Dawn.

Tracy suddenly smiled. She knew what to do about problems.

"I think we ought to ask Mr Tompsett," she said.

Mr Tompsett, when not actively care-taking, lived in a den down the steps by Class 1C's classroom door.

"I'll see if he's in," said Tania, and went to look. You could tell when Mr Tompsett was in by the wisps of tobacco smoke that seeped out under his door. And there was smoke seeping now as Tania looked.

"He's there," she called, and beckoned, keeping a watchful eye open for the Purgle. But Miss Purgletwitch was in no state to cause trouble: she was down in the staffroom, helping herself to some sherry left over from Christmas.

They marched down the steps one after the other, Tracy in front, carrying the box and feeling very important. She knocked politely at Mr Tompsett's door.

"Well, what do you want, you 'orrible brats?" said a voice. Tracy pushed open the door.

Mr Tompsett was sitting in his pink-striped deckchair, sipping a little refreshment from a Royal Wedding mug. Beside him on the table were his pipe, and a bottle of whisky labelled 'Mr Tompsett's Medicine'.

"It's only Us," said Tracy. "We've got a problem".

"A problem? Mmm . . ." Mr Tompsett took a thoughtful sip from his mug. "Well, take a pew," and he indicated the assorted mop-buckets with a regal wave of his hand.

Mr Tompsett's den was very cosy, thought Tracy, settling herself carefully on an upturned wastepaper basket. True, it was rather dim and murky, what with all the smoke and no windows. But he'd made an effort to make it feel like home. On the table there was a bright pink Busy Lizzie, to match the deckchair, and a budgerigar called Fosdyke in a cage.

"Well, what about this 'ere problem? What's up, luvie?"

Tracy cleared her throat.

"There was this egg," she began, "in a pineapple yoghurt carton," and she told him the whole story, with a little help from the others.

Mr Tompsett sat and listened quietly right to the end, though a flicker of something seemed to pass over his face when she got to the bit about Miss Purgletwitch diving under the desk. At the end he took a thoughtful swig from his Royal Wedding mug.

"So there's been a Hatching, and here you are with a baby thingummijig on your hands."

"That's it," said John.

"Well, 'ow I see it is this." Mr

24

Tompsett took a long pull on his pipe. "We've got this 'ere baby thingummijig, and we've got to do something about it, but we can't do nothing about it till we know what it is." He paused for comments, but everyone seemed to agree.

"I tell you what we need." Mr Tompsett leaned forward confidentially. "What we need is some o' them there books."

Rakesh and John and Jason hurried upstairs to the classroom library, while Tania and Dawn and Tracy peeped into the box to see how the baby thingummijig was doing. As they watched, he stirred and opened one green eye.

The boys soon returned with piles of books which they dumped down on the table next to Fosdyke the budgerigar. There was *Perfect Puppetry for the Complete Beginner*, and *New Maths, Book 5*, and several volumes of *Burton's Guide to Knowledge* — *Abacus to Artistotle*, *Arithmetic to Broomstick* and *Earwig to Emigration*.

Rakesh knew about indexes. He turned to the back of *Earwig to Emigration*. Mr Tompsett was impressed and watched admiringly over the rim of his cup.

"I read a book once," he said. "*Three Men in a Boat* it was called. That was in my younger days." He puffed on his pipe and sent smoke rings up to the ceiling.

"Eggs, that's what we need, Eggs," said Rakesh, trying to find page

2053. "Here we are . . . listen . . . 'Egg-apple: the fruit of the egg-plant. Egg-nog: a drink made of eggs and hot beer' . . ."

"That's a load of use," said John. Jason wasn't listening. He was busy searching through *Perfect Puppetry*, but couldn't find anything particularly helpful.

"Wait a bit," said Rakesh, getting quite worked up. "Here we are: 'Egg-slice: an implement for removing fried eggs from . . .'"

"I don't think that's it somehow," said Dawn.

"Why don't we look up Birds?" said Jason.

"Birds?"

"Well, he came from an egg, didn't he? Only birds come from eggs."

"Ah, there's birds and birds," said Mr Tompsett. "Look at his eyes now, green as jungles . . ."

But the boys were already deep in *Bat to Broomstick*. There was plenty about Bird-lime and Birds-of-a-feather and Birds'-nest-fern. John wanted to read out pages about the habits of hummingbirds, and had to be sat on by Tania. But as for wrinkled featherless birds with funny front legs like elbows and jungle green eyes . . .

"It's hopeless!" said Rakesh. "You'd think they'd never even HEARD of . . . of . . . baby thingummijigs."

"We certainly seem to be getting nowhere fast." Mr Tompsett leaned back in his deckchair. "Better give it up as a bad job."

"But what can we call him if we don't know what he is?"

"We'll 'ave to think up a name ourselves. Let's 'ave a good look at 'im now."

They all turned to look at the baby thingummijig, which had climbed to the top of the carton and was peering hopefully round the room.

"Told you he'd be hungry when he woke up," said Tracy.

"Let's 'ave a think," said Mr Tompsett. "Now, you could say he's sort of sludge coloured. Reckon maybe you ought to call him Sludge."

"Sludge?" Tracy and Dawn and Tania shook their heads.

"Something more sort of important," said Tracy thoughtfully.

"Let's 'ave a think," said Mr
Tompsett again. So they sat and had
a think, all screwed up and
squirming a bit, like you are if you're
thinking really hard. Rakesh
wrapped himself round a mop, and

Tania curled up against the table-
leg, and Tracy wriggled around on
the upturned wastepaper basket.
Only Mr Tompsett sat quite still,
leaning back in his deckchair and
puffing away at his pipe.

It was then in the silence that they heard it . . . a rustling, scrunching, scuffling, munching sound. The baby thingummijig had climbed out of his box and was tucking into *Burton's Guide to Knowledge*. Most of the first volume, *Abacus to Aristotle*, had already disappeared. The children leapt up from their thinking places.

"The book – it's nearly gone!"

"The Purgle'll kill us!"

"Told you he'd be hungry!" said Tracy and she popped him back in his newspaper nest and spoke rather sternly to him.

"Hey," said John, "look at that!" and he pointed to the remains of the book-binding, where *Aristotle* was spelt out in purple letters. "How about that for a name? It's a really long word!"

"Aristotle — it sounds very important," said Tracy.

"It is after all the VERY FIRST book he's eaten," said Rakesh.

"Better than calling him Abacus," said John.

"Aristotle — I like that," said Tania. "Aristotle Sludge. Hello, Mr Aristotle Sludge!"

The baby thingummijig stared at them with eyes that were as green as jungles.

"Mr Aristotle Sludge!"

Then he opened his mouth in what seemed to be a smile, as though he liked his name. Between his parted lips were two neat rows of teeth. And then they knew.

"That bird with teeth," said Dawn.

"That dinosaur bird," said Tania.

"Rather like lizards with wings . . ." muttered John. "Of course, of course!" and he leapt over the mop-bucket with a triumphant cry.

In mid-leap he twisted round and went rushing out of the door and up the stairs and along to the school canteen. He pushed past Class 1D who were waiting for seconds, and rushed right up to the hatch, where Mrs Cruickshank the dinner lady was serving chocolate pudding.

Mrs Cruickshank's face was usually flushed with the heat from the kitchen. But all the colour went from her cheeks as John blurted out his message.

"Steady on, you young scallywag.

Just you mind your language."

"But it's very important." John spoke very loudly, so all Class 1D could hear. "We need an extra big dinner. It's for our baby dinosaur."

"Ugh, what's that funny smell?" said Dawn a moment or two later.

Tracy wrinkled up her nose. "Something's off, if you ask me."

Just at that moment John appeared at the door, looking pleased with himself. There was a plate of dinner in his hand – fried mince and cabbage.

"For Mr Aristotle Sludge," he said proudly. He held the plate temptingly over the box so that Mr Sludge could enjoy the delicious smell.

"Sludgie, Sludgie, Sludgie! Come on, boy!" But Mr Sludge had retreated to the depths of the box, and was not to be moved.

"Oh come on, you!" John tapped the side of the box menacingly. Artistotle stayed hidden under the newspaper. John put a hand in to lift him out. This was too much for the baby dinosaur. He wriggled away from John's fingers, leapt clean out of his box, and retreated behind the bright pink Busy Lizzie.

"You're a nuisance, you are. You're the silliest dinosaur I've met," said John, putting the plate down in disgust.

"Perhaps," said Dawn thoughtfully, "perhaps he doesn't like cabbage. I mean, I don't like cabbage . . ."

"Nor me . . ."

"Nor me . . ."

"So perhaps . . ."

"Oh look everyone!" Tania cried out happily. "He likes me, look, he likes me!" And indeed, so it appeared, for Aristotle was heading straight for Tania, shuffling across the table with his funny front legs waggling around as he went.

"Hey, what do you want? What is it then?"

Aristotle had pushed his head into Tania's blazer pocket, which was just on a level with the table-top. And when he pulled his head out again, he had a bar of chocolate firmly grasped in his mouth.

"Hey, that's my tea you've got there!"

But that was the last Tania saw of her tea, for with a crunch and a gulp and a quick scuffle-munch, the chocolate was gone, wrapper and all. Then the baby dinosaur shuffled back to his box, was placed tenderly back amid the crumpled newspaper by Tracy, curled up tight and fell fast asleep.

Chapter Three

Mr Barnabas Blotting

They all jumped when the bell went for afternoon school.

Rakesh groaned. "Spellings, ugh!"

They thanked Mr Tompsett for his help, and made their way back to the classroom. Mr Sludge was sleeping peacefully in his cosy newspaper nest.

Miss Purgletwitch seemed to have made a fairly good recovery. But whenever she glanced at the cardboard box, she shuddered from head to toe.

The papers for the spelling test were given out, and the Purgle launched into number one, 'February'.

Now 'February' is hard to spell at the best of times. But it's even harder when you haven't had any lunch, and the space where your lunch should be is all vast and aching inside you. John managed alright, because he was good at spelling. But by the time they got to number 19, Tracy was feeling desperate.

"Number 20, hippopotamus . . . hippopot . . . And where do you think you're going, Tracy Browning?"

"Please Miss, it's Aristotle. He's squealing a bit, I think he's getting hungry . . ."

"SIT DOWN THIS MINUTE!"

So Tracy sat down. But she got her p's and t's in a nasty muddle as she listened to the sad whimpering from the cardboard box. He'll think we've let him down, she thought, and chewed her pencil miserably.

They got to number 27, 'Deciduous'. Tracy got up again and headed purposefully for the door.

"Tracy Browning, for the last time, this is NOT Piccadilly Circus . . ."

"Oh please, Miss! Poor Aristotle, he's so terribly hungry. And I think I've got some Smarties in my shoe-bag."

"You can't starve poor dumb creatures, miss," said John.

Jason looked at him admiringly.

"Oh, very well. But be QUICK!"

"Can I go with her, miss?"

"She may get lost on her own . . ."

"I think there's a Mars Bar he'd like in my anorak. Could I . . .?"

Miss Purgletwitch turned bright red and seemed to be winding herself up, like a clock that's about to strike. But just as she opened her mouth, there was a gentle knock at the classroom door.

"Do excuse me, Miss Purgletwitch." It was the school secretary, looking flustered. "This gentleman wants to see you. I told him you had a spelling test on, but he would insist."

The man whom she showed into

41

the classroom was clearly in a hurry. He kept looking anxiously from side to side, like one of those toy dogs with jointed heads that wobble. He was wearing a mustard coloured sports jacket and he had his left arm in a plaster cast, with something scrawled across it in bright pink letters. "Love from Miss Middleton," whispered John, who could read upside down.

The man swept breezily past the children's desks, sending spelling tests flying in all directions.

As soon as he arrived at the front of the class he grabbed Miss Purgletwitch's hand and shook it vigorously.

"Delighted to meet you, Miss Murglescratch." He spoke very

quickly in a high-pitched voice, like a
tape that's running too fast. Miss
Purgletwitch managed to get away,
and retreated behind her desk.

"Well, hello there children," he
went on, turning to the class. "I'd
better introduce myself. I'm
Barnabas Blotting – from the
Middleton Gazette, and I've heard
about the Hatching." He pulled a
wodge of paper from his pocket, and
rested it carefully on the plaster cast.

"Now, first of all I'd like to speak to the Finder. Which of you young ladies and gentlemen was it?" He looked around the class with greedy excited eyes.

Everyone turned to Tracy, who had slipped back into the classroom, and was secretly feeding Smarties to Mr Sludge. Tracy went to stand in front of the class, blushing and feeling very important.

"Well, hello there, young lady," he said, and patted her on the head. "So you were the Finder, were you? And what's your name?"

"Tracy Browning," said Tracy.

"And where was it that you found this – er – er – Egg?"

"In a giant pineapple yoghurt carton," said Tracy.

"Fascinating, that's really fascinating," said Barnabas Blotting, raising one eyebrow slightly. His pen squeaked horribly as he scribbled away. "And what about the Hatching? Could you tell me what kind of a creature it is?"

"We couldn't tell," said Tracy. "He was so big for a baby. But then he started to smile, and that's when we knew for sure."

"Knew for sure?" said Mr Blotting, above the squeak of his pen. "Knew what for sure?"

"Knew that he was a dinosaur, of course," said Tracy. Miss Purgletwitch sat down rather suddenly.

"Mmm . . . well, thank you, thank you very much, Miss Browning." He patted her on the head again, which made Tracy cross. She sat down, trying to look as grown-up as possible. "Now could anyone fill me in a bit about this species? I mean, we don't come across dinosaurs every day."

John stood up. "That's because they've been extinct for millions of years, sir, you see. This particular dinosaur belongs to the group pterosaurus, otherwise known as pterodactyls, an extinct order of flying reptiles, prevalent in the Jurassic and Cretaceous periods . . ." He paused for breath. Mr Blotting ran out of paper, and started to write on his plaster cast.

"This species," John went on, "was characterized by . . ."

"Thank you, thank you very

much, young man, that's really
fascinating," said Mr Blotting,
flexing his right wrist which was
quite painful from all the writing.
"That really fills me in from that
angle. Now, could someone tell me
how you're going to look after your
ptero . . . your dinosaur? What are
you going to feed him on, for
instance?"

Tania stood up bravely. "He likes
chocolate," she said. Her voice went
all husky, like it always did when
she was nervous. "Chocolate and
encyclopedias."

"Encyclopedias?" Mr Blotting's
eyebrow went up even further.

"Oh yes, he ate the first volume of
Burton's Guide to Knowledge." Miss
Purgletwitch went rather pale. Tania

noticed and faltered slightly. "Well, not ALL of it . . . only as far as Aristotle."

"I see, I see, how fascinating." The plaster cast was quite filled up: the message from Miss Middleton was completely hidden. "Well, children, I think that will be all. Thank you children, thank you, Miss Gurglepatch . . ." and Mr Barnabas Blotting left the classroom at a trot, sending several more spelling tests flying as he went. When Miss Purgletwitch tried to get on with the spelling test, no one could find their piece of paper, so they had to do Drawing for the rest of the afternoon.

Before they went home that night, Tracy and Dawn and Mr Sludge

48

went down to see Mr Tompsett. Mr Tompsett was sitting in his deckchair, taking a little refreshment to strengthen himself for the evening's duties.

They told him all about Barnabas Blotting. Mr Tompsett was impressed.

"You'll be famous, mark my words," he said. "You're 'eading for the big time, that's what I say. And now what about the baby thingummijig? What happens to him now?"

"I wish I could take him home," said Tracy. "But Rex would have him for supper." Rex was the Brownings' poodle, and the terror of the neighbourhood.

"And my Mum doesn't like

animals," said Dawn. "So it's a Problem."

"Well, I've been thinking about this 'ere Problem." Mr Tompsett smiled rather smugly to himself. "And I think I may say as I've come up with an Answer."

He fished around under the table, and pulled out a big rusty birdcage.

"Used to belong to a parrot," he explained, dusting it out with his handkerchief. "Fosdyke lived in it, till I got 'im a brand new budgie cage. Just the job for the baby thingummijig. You leave 'im 'ere with me, he'll be safe as 'ouses."

Tracy picked up the contents of the box, newspaper, dinosaur and all, and put them in the birdcage. Then they got together all the food they could find – the rest of the Smarties, and some of Dawn's liquorice allsorts, and three jaffa cakes that Mr Tompsett dug out from the depths of his overalls.

"Should keep him going till tomorrow," said Tracy. "Goodnight, then, Mr Sludge." She poked a

finger between the bars and gently scratched his head. He looked up at her with green eyes and made a wild little cry a bit like a seagull's wail.

Chapter Four

What Happened Behind The Bicycle Sheds

"They're having us on!" Tracy's father propped his newspaper against the Cornflakes packet. "These lying journalists can't be trusted an inch. Just listen to this:
BLAST FROM THE PAST AT MIDDLETON SCHOOL.
"Kids at Middleton School had the Shock of their lives yesterday, when

an adorable Dinosaur Chick hatched out on their Nature Table. Cute little Tracy Browning, the Finder of the egg, told me . . ." Tracy Browning? Tracy Browning!! Tracy! Come here! What the . . .?"

But Tracy had grabbed her bag and fled, and was halfway up the road.

When she had arrived safely at school, Tracy went straight to Mr Tompsett's den.

"How is he? Is he alright? Did he miss me?"

"'E's alright, don't fret yourself, luvie." Mr Tompsett was sitting peacefully in his deckchair, enjoying a quiet smoke. "Mind you, 'e looked in a bad way this morning. Could be 'e's hungry, I thought to meself. Got through 'is tea by five o'clock last evening, the little Tartar." Mr Tompsett chuckled. "But I gave 'im a sip of whisky, 'n' 'e perked up pretty quick."

The sip of whisky certainly seemed to have worked. Mr Aristotle Sludge was shuffling happily round his cage, waggling his funny front legs. Tracy had a good look at him.

"Hey, Mr Tompsett, d'you think he's grown? I'm sure he's bigger than yesterday!"

"Who knows?" said Mr Tompsett. He leaned back in his deckchair, smoking thoughtfully. "You never can tell with dinosaurs," he added, but just at that moment the bell went, and Tracy didn't hear. She hurried up the stairs to the

classroom, the dinosaur cage
clutched carefully under her arm.

It was Science to start with. Normally
Tracy liked Science. But that
morning she found it hard to
concentrate. What was more, the
Purgle was in a difficult mood. She

56

shouted at Dawn for no good reason at all: just because Dawn went to see how Mr Sludge was doing. When Tracy tried to get some Smarties from the cloakroom, the Purgle put her to work on her own in the Quiet Room. And when John asked if they could get on with their dinosaur pictures, she turned quite pale and talked very fast about tadpoles.

At playtime the six gathered round to discuss the problem.

"It's just not on," said Tracy. "There's so much we've got to do. There's feeding him and talking to him and cleaning out his cage. But we'll never manage it, while the Purgle keeps pestering."

"She's always going on about Nature," said John. "And now she's got a bit of Nature under her very eyes, and she doesn't want to know."

"She's a PEST," said Jason, and brought his fist hard down on the table, like people do in films. Unfortunately it hurt more than he intended.

"I think she's sort of scared," said Dawn shyly, but no one heard.

"We'll have to get her out of the way," said Rakesh darkly.

"I've got it," cried John suddenly, giving Jason a gleeful punch. "A Committee, that's what we need — we'll have to hold a Committee." But just then the bell went and they couldn't find out what he meant.

After playtime it was Long Multiplication. John was very quick at multiplication so he finished before everyone else and had plenty of time to spare. He wrote out a notice in red felt-tip and passed it round the table.

"ATTENTION, the Sludge Committee. Meeting today at lunch-time behind the bicycle sheds. B.A.B.O.C."

"That means Bring A Bottle Of Coke," hissed John, leaning across to Rakesh.

Jason stared at the piece of paper, rather puzzled.

"The Sludge Committee – who's that?" he whispered behind his pencil-case to Rakesh.

"US, silly," said Rakesh.

Jason had never been on a Committee before. It made him feel several inches taller. He gave up on

the sums, and stared out of the
window, lost in happy dreams.

And so at 12 o'clock prompt the
Sludge Committee, armed with coke
and crisps, met behind the bicycle
sheds. Aristotle Sludge was fast
asleep in the safety of Mr Tompsett's
den.

"First of all," said John, settling
himself on the grass, "what we need
is a Chairperson." John knew about

Committees. His mother was on
several, and had outfits to match —
an Indian dress for Save the Whales,
and a boiler suit for the Film Society,
and blue dungarees for the Whole-
Food Co-op.

"Who'll be Chairperson then?"
said Rakesh hopefully.

"I'll be it if you like," said John.
Rakesh munched fiercely through
his handful of crisps.

"Now who's going to take the
Minutes?" said John. "You always
have to have someone to take the
Minutes. My mum's always going on
about it."

"I've got a new watch," said Jason
helpfully.

"Right then," said John. "That's
your job, taking the Minutes."

Jason looked at his watch in a rather puzzled way.

"Ladies and gentlemen," said John, "we are here today to discuss the dinosaur problem: or What To Do With Mr Aristotle Sludge." He paused for comments.

"The Purgle'll have to learn," said Tracy darkly after a while. "I mean, there ARE limits."

"She gets all excited about things in books," said Rakesh, "but she doesn't seem to like it when things are Real."

"I think she's sort of scared," said Dawn again, but no one heard her.

"It's too much to expect. We can't look after him and go to lessons as well," said Tania.

"And we've got our public to think

of," said John. "I mean, after all, with that in the papers, word'll get round. We'll probably have to give lots of interviews."

"There's something else," said Tracy. "I spent all my pocket money on chocolate this morning. And he's finished it off already. What about all the food he needs? Where's it going to come from?"

"It's a Problem," said Dawn.

There was silence for a while, broken only by the munching of crisps.

"Come on Jason, you say something," said John.

Jason was still staring at his watch. He looked up suddenly and saw everyone looking at him. He went rather red.

"Well, I s'pose," he said, "well, how about . . . um . . . couldn't we make the classroom into a mu . . . you know, one of those places where people go to see things?"

Everyone stared at Jason with wide-open eyes.

"A museum?" said John. And then "A MUSEUM!" and he jumped up and hit Jason so hard that Jason turned a somersault. "That's it, don't you see? A museum! The Aristotle Sludge Museum!"

"We'd have to make people pay," said Tracy.

"20p for entrance – coke and crisps extra."

"We'd make lots of money!"

"Pensioners half-price . . ."

"Double-price for Class 1D!"

"We'd have to have other things to show," said Jason.

"My spiders' eggs!"

"My Spanish shawl!"

"My dogs' teeth I found on the building site!"

"Come on, everybody," said John, "let's go and see Mr Flinch."

And off they all marched to the Headmaster's office, with Jason at their head. Jason was the hero of the hour. Everybody forgave him for forgetting to take the Minutes.

Chapter Five

"There's Wings and Wings"

The Headmaster wasn't surprised by the plan. He'd been working at Middleton School for years and was never surprised by anything. He heard the children through, then shook his head in a tired way and sent them away. The children were disappointed but there was nothing they could do. They dropped in to tell Mr Tompsett on the way back to class.

Just before lunch Jason was stacking some books in a cupboard in the corridor. The corridor was empty, except for Mr Tompsett, who was mopping up some spilt paint and humming to himself.

Jason didn't hear the Headmaster coming. Mr Flinch walked very quietly in his soft-soled shoes. So if you were doing something wrong, you never had time to stop.

"Morning," said the Headmaster. Jason jumped. But Mr Flinch was talking to Mr Tompsett.

"Morning, Mr Flinch." Mr Tompsett carried on with his mopping, then suddenly stopped, as though he'd just thought of something. "Oh, Mr Flinch, sir, I just wondered if you'd caught sight of this."

He pulled a press cutting from the pocket of his overalls, shook off the jaffa cake crumbs and held it out at arm's length.

"BLAST FROM THE PAST AT MIDDLETON SCHOOL."

Mr Tompsett rolled his tongue round the words. The Headmaster shifted from foot to foot. "Kids at Middleton School had the shock of their Lives yesterday, when an adorable Dinosaur Chick . . ."

"That's enough," said Mr Flinch. There was a twitch at the side of his mouth. Jason could tell that he'd read the paper.

"Well, sir," said Mr Tompsett,

folding up the cutting thoughtfully, "I wouldn't be in your shoes today for anything. You must feel everyone's got their eyes on you, they must be wondering just what's going on at Middleton School."

"Well, er, yes, I expect they are," said Mr Flinch, shuddering slightly as he remembered a phone call from one of Her Majesty's Inspectors at half-past eight that morning.

"You must be right worried about it all," Mr Tompsett went on. "I don't envy you your job one bit, that I don't . . . Mind you, every cloud 'as a silver lining, and it's an ill wind that blows nobody good."

"Well, er," said Mr Flinch, shifting from one foot to the other.

"That's it, sir. You know how to

handle this kind of bother, you'll make the best of it. I mean, I gather it's all the rage now, kids doing their own thing. Projects, they call 'em, don't they? Could be you'll be the very first school with a real live prehistorical project."

"Not if I can help it," said Mr Flinch.

Mr Tompsett shook his head. "That's you all over, sir, too modest by half. I mean, you've got a name already, sir, for your displays and suchlike."

Mr Flinch stopped frowning and nodded thoughtfully. "I'm not saying these new ideas are all bad," he said. "It's just important not to get carried away."

"I know what you mean, Mr

Flinch, sir. But you can do it, sir, you'll show you're still in charge." Mr Tompsett waved the press cutting in the air to get the point across. "You're already a trendsetter, sir. You hear people talking about it, they're always going on about the displays at Middleton School."

Mr Flinch scratched his head.
"I suppose there might be something
to be said for it," he said. "A little
experiment, perhaps. The children
doing some work on their own and
making a display and inviting their
parents and friends in to share it.
Making their very own little
museum, you might say."

"Ah, I wouldn't know about that,"
said Mr Tompsett. "I wouldn't know
about how you'd go about it. All
those finer points are lost on me."

"Mind you," said Mr Flinch,
"I shall have to square it with the
governors. That could be a problem
— they're a little stick-in-the-mud, so
to speak, our Board of Governors."

"You'll manage that, sir. You'll
know how to put it to them — so they

almost think they've thought up the idea themselves. Just you remember, sir. Every cloud has a silver lining. But not every school has a dinos . . ."

"Ow," said Jason. Two atlases had fallen on his foot. The Headmaster turned and noticed him, and went off down the corridor with Mr Tompsett, so Jason never heard the end of the conversation.

That afternoon the Headmaster called the children back into his office. He explained he'd been thinking about their plan, and he'd decided to let them give it a try.

And so it was settled. Miss Purgletwitch went off to Tunisia for an extended holiday. Those children in Class 1C who weren't particularly interested went off to join Class 1A, 1B or 1D. And the Sludge Committee were left to themselves – with a helping hand now and then from Mr Tompsett.

"First," said John, "we've got to put up a Notice. When people come to see something, they want to know where they've come to."

So Rakesh and Tania, who were good at letters, made a great banner out of a roll of wallpaper. It said "THE ARISTOTLE SLUDGE MUSEUM" in shiny letters a metre high. They pinned it over the classroom door and it looked splendid – even though it did occasionally come adrift and hit unwary visitors over the head.

The next morning the children

brought their treasures to be displayed. The arranging of exhibits was by no means an easy task. There was a lot of debate over some of the items. Opinions were divided, for instance, on Rakesh's dogs' teeth. There was some feeling that they held little interest for the general public. They were, as Dawn pointed out, so very tooth-like, and also rather muddy. But after a quick scrub with Mr Tompsett's toothbrush they looked much more attractive.

Jason's dead frog, however, posed no problem. Everyone approved, and it was given pride of place next to Tania's plastic daffodils. There was agreement, too, on the appeal of Rakesh's model turtle, and Dawn's coloured duck that said "Happy Christmas from Clacton". Tracy's ball-bearings were felt to be too precious to go on display. "Specially with Class 1D on the warpath," said Rakesh.

When Mr Tompsett produced his famous collection of postcards bought on a seaside holiday in Blackpool, all work came to a standstill for a time. They were pored over at length and highly praised. Then they were pinned to the notice board, next to Tracy's Spanish shawl. But it was agreed that they would be removed if John's mother decided to visit.

"She'd say they were sexist. No sense of humour, my Mum," said John sadly, carefully arranging

Tracy's shells next to Rakesh's spiders' eggs in their red bucket.

It was John himself who caused the greatest problem. His contribution to the museum was a stuffed fox.

"Great-grandad shot it in Scotland in 1911," he said proudly. "You have to be careful with it. It's rather rotten."

But it was only a few minutes later that disaster struck. Jason was standing on tiptoe on a chair, trying to place the fox on the shelf on top of the blackboard. Unfortunately, the floor had been polished only the night before. As Jason stretched up, the chair slipped, and Jason lost his footing. Down he came crashing, fox and all. Jason only bruised his elbow.

The fox however was not so lucky. As it hit the floor it dissolved in a cloud of dust. For days there were little bits of fox floating in the air. It brought on Mr Tompsett's hayfever, and he had to retire downstairs for a little refreshment.

Mr Aristotle Sludge watched all the arrangements with interest – especially of course the eating arrangements. The desk that had been Miss Purgletwitch's was turned into the museum canteen. There were crisps and peanuts and biscuits for sale, double price for Class 1D. There was coffee too: Tania had got Mrs Cruickshank on her side and borrowed a hot water urn, which fizzled and spat encouragingly. The money for all the refreshments came from the Sludge Fund, set up at Mr Tompsett's suggestion – half of everyone's pocket money went into the Fund, which was used to buy Aristotle's food as well as biscuits for visitors. Rakesh, who had a pocket calculator, was chosen to be Treasurer. He hid the money away in an empty marmalade pot in Mr Tompsett's den, and went round all day fiddling with his calculator and looking very important.

The day wore on. At last tea-time came and the Sludge Committee headed for home, with the sort of appetite you only get after making a museum. Tracy was the last to leave. She was just going out of the door when she heard a crash. She turned;

the Spanish shawl had come
tumbling down and brought half the
seaside postcards with it.

"Flying fishsticks!" said Tracy.
"It'll take hours to put them back."
But the Opening was tomorrow.
There was nothing for it.

It was quiet in the classroom after
all the noise of the day. Warm too,
thought Tracy: sticking in drawing
pins is surprisingly hot work. She
went to open the window.

A good smell came flooding in
from outside, the smell of grass after
rain. It made you think of buttercups
and wet green things, the sort of
things you forget about in hot chalky
classrooms. Tracy took a deep
breath. It made her feel like Spring.
She would walk home slowly. She

went back to pinning up the postcards.

Tracy had nearly finished her job when she heard it. Scritter-scratter, scritch-scratch, scritter-scratter-scratter. She put down the drawing pins and listened. Scritter-scrat. It seemed to be coming from Aristotle's cage. Tracy crept over and peered inside.

"Flying fishsticks," said Tracy.

Aristotle Sludge was dancing a war dance. Round and round he went in a clumsy shuffle, flicking his tail and waggling his funny front legs in the air. Wildly he went here and there through the crumpled newspaper, stamping his feet and flashing his gleaming green eyes. And now and then he wailed a weird little wail, like a gull in a storm.

Tracy tiptoed out of the room.
She could hear the swish of Mr
Tompsett's mop.

"Mr Tompsett," she called softly.
"Mr Tompsett, come here!"

Mr Tompsett came. Together they
stood quite still, and stared at the
dinosaur's dance.

"What's he up to?" said Tracy. "Why's he doing it, Mr Tompsett?"

"Could be 'e's stretchin' 'is wings," said Mr Tompsett.

"Wings? You mean those elbow things? They aren't proper wings. He'll never be able to get anywhere on those."

"Ah, there's wings and wings." Mr Tompsett leaned on his mop and looked wise. "Hark at 'is cry now — wild as storm winds! Spring's got into 'im, you mark my words."

Chapter Six

Some Visitors

At nine o'clock next morning the
Aristotle Sludge Museum was
officially opened. They celebrated
with Coke all round, a sip of whisky
for Mr Tompsett, and a giant bar of
fruit and nut chocolate for Aristotle
Sludge himself.

One of the very first visitors was
the Headmaster. Mr Tompsett said
they should let him in without

paying, though John would much have preferred to charge him double.

"We can't do that, now can we?" said Mr Tompsett. "After all, 'e did give us the premises."

So John gave in, and they let Mr Flinch in free, and gave him a coffee and two gingernuts.

"So this is the famous dinosaur," he said, peering over his spectacles. "Pterosaurus, I see — dating from — er — several million years ago."

"The Jurassic period to be precise," said John who was standing near. The Headmaster stared at John. For once he looked slightly surprised. "Though some remains do survive from the Cretaceous period," John went on.

The Headmaster's knees gave way and he sat down suddenly on the dead frog. He got up again equally quickly.

"This species," John added, "was characterized by . . ." and he stopped. The Headmaster had rushed off, suddenly recalling a very urgent appointment. "It's funny," said John to Jason. "He's just like the Purgle. He's always going on about reading books and things. But he doesn't seem to like it when things are Real."

The Headmaster was closely followed by a group from Class 1D. They made straight for Mr Sludge's cage.

"Don't see what all the fuss is about."

"Ugh, he's all sludgey and brown."

"Not much bigger than a lizard."

But although they pretended not to be impressed, they hung around for quite a while, and one or two of them backed away when he bared his teeth.

The next visitors were a group of people on their way home from the shops. Tania's Dad was there: the factory where he'd worked had closed down, and now he stayed home and looked after the babies. He'd brought along one of Tania's little sisters.

"Tish see dwagon! Tish see dwagon!" she sang out happily from her push-chair.

"She means dragon," explained Tania. "Listen, Trisha, it's not a

dragon, it's a dinosaur."

Trisha was taken to peer in the cage. Mr Aristotle Sludge poked his nose out of the newspaper and winked at her. Trisha clapped her hands.

"Tish see dwagon!"

"It's not a dragon. Dragons aren't REAL!" said John scornfully. "You only get them in fairy stories. That's kids' stuff – not like dinosaurs."

But Tania's sister was not to be convinced. She was wheeled out crowing happily. "Tish see dwagon! Tish see dwagon!"

It was about this time that the only awkward moment occurred. Kevin Jones from Class 1D was caught slipping Jason's dead frog up his sleeve. Jason was all for vengeance, and grabbed the nearest pair of compasses. But Mr Tompsett felt this was going too far. He merely took his mop in one hand, and politely asked Kevin Jones to leave the room. Mr Tompsett could look quite menacing when he chose. Kevin left, his face the colour of squashy tomatoes.

Then came Mr Crumpsall, who taught at the local college. He slapped John on the shoulder in a friendly way.

"Friend of my Mum's," hissed John to Jason. "They're on a Committee together, the Ban-the-Spaghetti-Streak-Committee."

Jason looked puzzled. "Why do they want to ban spaghetti?"

"Not spaghetti, stupid! Spaghetti Streak, this new supersonic plane they're always going on about on the telly. Flying faster than sound from London to Naples. My Mum and old Crumps here think it's dangerous — they're trying to get it banned. Old Crumps made up a slogan about it! 'Jobs Not Bangs'. They reckon all sorts of buildings might get damaged."

"What about school buildings?" said Jason hopefully.

"Not likely, stupid," said John. "They're worried about old buildings, churches and things."

"Ah," said Jason, rapidly losing interest.

Mr Crumpsall wandered round the museum, smiling and saying how interesting everything was. Smiling, that is, till he saw Rakesh's dogs' teeth, when he left in a hurry.

Just before lunchtime some reporters arrived. There were three of them this time, and they came from the local television company. They all smoked cigars and had complicated cameras. They took lots of pictures of Mr Aristotle Sludge, and Tracy had to answer questions

into a microphone. Tracy was
getting good at dealing with
reporters. Nobody now would have
dreamt of patting her on the head.

At twelve o'clock sharp they shut
for lunch. Tania finished washing

the coffee cups and sank into Miss Purlgetwitch's chair with a sigh.

"My feet hurt," she groaned.

But when Rakesh had worked out their profits on his pocket calculator she brightened up a lot.

"Six pounds forty," he shouted. "We're going places, folks! I'll have to find another marmalade pot to keep it in."

Chapter Seven

Moving House

For the next few days they were very busy indeed. They had a steady stream of visitors, among them the lollipop lady, and Mr Hodge from the Fish 'n' Chip shop, and Jason's Dad looking very smart in his bus-conductor's uniform, and the man who sold hot dogs. John's mother came too, in the Indian dress she wore for Save The Whales. Fortunately John spotted her just in time, and hung the Spanish shawl across the seaside postcards. Everyone seemed to enjoy themselves, though Mr Hodge turned out to be scared of spiders, and had to be calmed down by Mr Tompsett after going a bit too near the red plastic bucket.

When the story made headlines in the national newspapers, people began to arrive from farther away. On Thursday there was a minibus full of bird-lovers from Birmingham, complete with binoculars. There was quite a queue to get in.

They'd just got the last of the bird-lovers into the museum, and Rakesh's third marmalade pot was filling up nicely, when there was a sudden shriek.

"Flying fishsticks! He's stuck!" The plastic daffodils quivered at the sound, and all the seaside postcards fell off the wall.

It was Tracy over by Aristotle's cage. Everyone turned and stared. The other children pushed through the crowded museum to see what was happening.

"Poor old Aristotle!"

Tracy had been feeding Aristotle his third chocolate bar of the day. But in his enthusiasm, he'd pushed his head too far out between the bars and got stuck. He stared up

helplessly at the children with sad green eyes.

"Get some soap somebody quick!"

Dawn was soon on hand with some smelly pink soap from the toilets. The visitors gathered round, fascinated. With a bit of lathering and a lot of pushing and pulling the children at last succeeded in setting Aristotle free. He munched his way through the chocolate, looking rather miserable.

The children tried to carry on as if nothing had happened, but all of them seemed very thoughtful. Just before lunchtime, John passed round a notice which read: "Attention: the Sludge Committee. Meeting at 12.15 sharp in the museum canteen."

98

So, as soon as the museum closed for lunch, the children gathered on, at and under the table that had been Miss Purgletwitch's.

John put on his important committee voice. "We are here today, ladies and gentlemen, to discuss a Problem: the Problem being that Sludge's cage has got far too small. Could I have some suggestions from the Floor?"

Jason was sitting under the table, and thought John must mean him.

"We could make a bigger one," he said helpfully.

"How?" said Tracy. "It looks ever so difficult."

"Easy peasy," said Rakesh, who'd made a book-end once. "Easy peasy if only we had some wood."

"Where could we get it from?"

"Wood's very dear, my Dad says," added Tania.

"We could chop up the desks," said Jason from under the table.

"There must be an answer," said John. "Hey, Mr Tompsett, what d'you think? Mr Tompsett?"

But Mr Tompsett was nowhere to be seen.

"Just when we need him," said Tracy crossly.

"We'll have to save up for some wood, there's nothing else for it," said John.

"But in the meantime he'll go on getting stuck," said Tania.

Everybody's face fell.

"Poor old Aristotle!"

"It's a Problem," said Dawn.

Just at that moment Mr Tompsett reappeared. He sat down next to the dead frog, puffing thoughtfully at his pipe.

"Mr Tompsett, what should we do?" said Tracy.

"Well, 'ow I see it is this," said Mr Tompsett. "We 'aven't got any wood. But we need a cage, a very big cage. Now 'ow can you make a cage without any wood?"

"You can't," said John.

"We've been into all that already," said Rakesh.

"Where there's a will there's a way," said Mr Tompsett.

"We could chop up the desks," said Jason again, through a mouthful of crisps.

The children looked round the

classroom in despair. Then suddenly Tania jumped to her feet. "The Quiet Room. Why don't we use the Quiet Room?"

Everyone turned to stare at the little reading room behind Miss Purgletwitch's desk.

"Don't you see? We could fence it off."

"She's right — all we'd need is some wire netting."

"He'd have bags of room in there!"

"He could dance around as much as he liked!"

"Good old Tania!"

"How does that sound, Mr Sludge?" said Tracy.

The dinosaur opened one eye and winked at her, then settled down cosily again in the *Middleton Gazette*.

Mr Tompsett smiled. "What did I tell you? Where there's a will there's a way. And it just so 'appens I've got a role of chickenwire goin' spare downstairs. I was just wonderin' when it was goin' to come in 'andy."

They decided to close the museum for the afternoon. They made a large notice and stuck it to the door. "SORRY – SHUT FOR ALTERATIONS. BUSINESS AS USUAL TOMORROW." John chose the words for the notice and everyone agreed it sounded very official.

Then Mr Tompsett, Rakesh, John and Tania set to work to fence off the Quiet Room. Meanwhile, Tracy,

Dawn and Jason cleared out the room itself, and tried to make it into a comfortable home. They were running out of *Middleton Gazettes*, so they decided he'd have to make do with crumpled egg-boxes. There was no shortage of egg-boxes. There are always plenty of egg-boxes in classroom cupboards.

"It doesn't look too comfortable," said Dawn.

"He'll manage," said Tracy. "He's tough, old Aristotle. His skin's getting all sort of leathery now."

Then they found a few branches that had been blown down on the playing field. They scattered these round the room, "to make it more lifelike," as Dawn said.

Finally Mr Tompsett put down his

hammer with a satisfied sigh.

"There we are then," he said.
They stood back to admire their
handiwork. The chickenwire was
tacked down firmly across the Quiet
Room entrance. There was a door
on a frame, just as tall as Tracy.

"Well done, us!" said John.

"It's beautiful!" said Tracy.
"A proper house. How d'you like
that, Aristotle, old thing?" And she
opened the cage and lifted him out
into his huge new home.

The little dinosaur went wild with
delight. He tore around through the
egg-boxes, stamping his clawed feet
and waving his elbows in the air.
Then suddenly he scrabbled his way
up one of the branches. At the top
he paused, looking round. A strange

gleam came into his jungle-green
eyes. And then he threw himself
off . . . flump – crunch into the
crumpled egg-boxes.

"Silly old Sludge! What ARE you
up to?" said Tania.

But Aristotle was not in the least
put off by his crash-landing. Up he
went again to the top of the branch,
and down again – flump – crunch.

"What on earth's he doing? Mr
Tompsett, what's he doing?"

"Practice," said Mr Tompsett,
briefly.

"What d'you mean?" said Rakesh.

"Like I said, practice. Getting in
some practice for the Big Day."

The Alterations had taken the whole
afternoon and Mr Tompsett had got

behind with his cleaning.

"Can I stay and help you?" Tracy asked, when all the others had gone home. "Mum's on early shift this week, so I don't have to get back to make the tea."

"Well now, that would be nice of you, luvie. Much appreciated, that would be." He gave her some polish and a duster, and she set to work to bring up a shine on the museum canteen table.

As Tracy worked away, she heard the wind rising outside. Sounds like a storm, she thought, I'd better go home by the short cut. Down the corridor Mr Tompsett was whistling, like he always did when a storm was on the way. And from the Quiet Room came the sound of Mr

Sludge's war-dance . . . scritter-scratter scritch-scratch scritter-scratter scritch-scratch, regular in the stillness. Then suddenly it stopped.

Curious, Tracy went to peep through the chickenwire. The dinosaur was perched on the window sill, staring out at the darkening sky. Outside, the kitchen lady was putting out the dustbins. A flock of seagulls soared over the playground, wheeling and diving down in search of scraps. Their white wings flashed against the storm-clouds. Aristotle perched on the windowsill and stared, and every now and then he uttered his wild little wail.

I do believe he wants to be with

them, Tracy thought, and softly she called to Mr Tompsett.

Together they stood quite still and watched, while Aristotle Sludge stared out at the bright wings in the storm.

"D'you think it's fair, Mr Tompsett?" whispered Tracy. "D'you think it's fair to keep him shut up like this? I mean, now he's a baby and needs to be looked after . . . but one day he'll be able to look after himself . . ."

"Ah, don't you worry, luvie," said Mr Tompsett. "Could be 'e'll take 'imself off when the time's ripe. Could be you won't be able to keep 'im." He leant on his mop and rubbed his right ear thoughtfully. "You never can tell with dinosaurs," he added.

Then Tracy asked a question that had been troubling her for days.

"Where d'you think he came from, Mr Tompsett? How did the egg get into the yoghurt carton?"

"Well, I don't rightly know, luvie. Though I've 'ad me thoughts on the subject. I got a 'phone call from this old girl the other week. So off I went to see 'er in 'er queer old house. It was all dark and spider-webby, and cluttered up to the eyeballs with this 'n' that. This old girl 'ad all these things she wanted to give the school, old books and paints and brushes and what-not. I couldn't refuse them, now could I?"

Tracy stared. "You mean, that's where the egg came from? D'you think she slipped it in with all the other things? Mr Tompsett, d'you think she meant us to find it?"

Mr Tompsett shrugged. "I wouldn't know, luvie. That's a tricky question, that one."

"But it's ever so odd, isn't it?" Tracy frowned. "I mean, he's the very first dinosaur for an awfully long time."

"Ah, there's time and time," said Mr Tompsett.

"What d'you mean?" said Tracy.

"Well," said Mr Tompsett, rubbing his right ear, "there's ordinary sorts of time, past and present and future, what-was-and-is-and-will-be, as you might say. And then there's what's going on behind all that."

"Ah," said Tracy, not quite understanding.

"Your Mr Sludge now," went on Mr Tompsett, "where does he belong? P'raps he don't belong to what-was-and-is-and-will-be . . .

Look at his eyes now, green as jungles!"

"Why d'you always say that?" said Tracy. "There aren't any jungles round here now."

"Ah," said Mr Tompsett, "that there aren't." He went back to his mopping.

Chapter Eight

"You Never Can Tell With Dinosaurs"

Next morning John burst into the museum full of excitement. "Anyone see Spaghetti Streak on the telly?"

"Spaghetti what?" Dawn looked confused.

"Spaghetti Streak – the supersonic jet – my mum's on the Committee, you know — and they're trying it out today . . ."

"And we're right in the flight path, my Dad said," added Rakesh.

"Jobs Not Bangs, Jobs Not Bangs," chanted John.

There was a loud knock at the door.

"Flying fishsticks!" said Tracy.

Everyone jumped. Jason looked hopefully for cracks in the walls.

But it was no supersonic jet — only the school secretary. "I've just had a phone-call," she said. "I felt you should know straight away. It was from Professor Baffle: he says he wants to visit."

"Is he Very Important?" said Tracy. When Very Important Visitors came, the museum was closed to others. For visitors who were only Important, business went on as usual.

"I thought you'd want to know," said the secretary, "so I took some notes from *Who's Who*." She pulled a paper from her pocket and took a deep breath. "'BAFFLE: Alfred Charles. World authority on the pterosaurus, the woolly mammoth, and other extinct species. Specialist in dentition'."

"Dent what?" said Jason.

"Teeth, silly," said John. "Like dentists."

"He's written several books," the secretary went on. "*Some Fossils of the Cretaceous Period*, and *Some Aspects of Cretaceous Dentition* and *Tooth and Claw in the Jurassic Jungle*." The secretary ran out of breath and sat down suddenly on the dead frog. She got up equally quickly.

"He sounds Very Important Indeed," said Tania, impressed.

"Does it say if he's scared of spiders?" said Rakesh anxiously, remembering an awkward moment with Mr Hodge from the Fish 'n' Chip shop, but the secretary had vanished, suddenly remembering some business she had to attend to.

"Action stations, folks," said John.

So Tania turned on the hot-water urn, and Rakesh went to dust the plastic daffodils, and Jason went to inspect the seaside postcards. And Mr Tompsett was called in to assist.

"What on earth is Mr Sludge up

to?" said Tania suddenly. "He's really wild today."

"Doing his war-dance," said John. They went to watch.

The dinosaur was careering round the cage, flinging himself from the branches, whirling around like a storm-wind, with powdered egg-boxes smoking out behind him.

"He's getting ever so big," said Tracy, looking worried. She remembered Mr Tompsett's words: "Perhaps you'll find you won't be able to keep him . . ." She stared at the dancing dinosaur. "He really isn't a baby any more . . . Flying fishsticks, what's going on?"

There was a sudden roar from outside. Aristotle leapt to the window-sill, wailing a wild jungle-wail. With a whistling and whirring of rotor blades a helicopter touched down on the playing-field.

"It's ruined the football pitch!"

"That'll be him," cried Tania.

She went to get the notice that said "SORRY: CLOSED FOR VERY IMPORTANT PERSON." It was hidden under some packets of crisps, and it took her a while to find it. She went to pin the notice to the door.

"Sorry," she said to a man who was waiting there. He was a dumpy little man in a fading yellow cardigan and baggy trousers. He looked bedraggled but friendly, like a muddy spaniel. "Sorry, we're shut". She pointed to the notice.

The man looked disappointed.

His mouth twitched, but the words wouldn't come out. He stared at her through his thick gold-rimmed spectacles. Tania wondered if he'd come to clean the windows.

"Come back after lunch," she said helpfully. "This morning, we're waiting for Professor Baffle."

"Oh," said the man. He nodded and turned to go. Then suddenly he stopped and looked anxiously at Tania over his shoulder. "But Professor Baffle is me," he said.

"Do come in, Professor," said John over Tania's shoulder, as Tania tried to disappear into the doorpost. "Welcome to our Museum." John was good with university people: there were several in his mother's Wholefood Co-op. He led the

Professor into the classroom.

Professor Baffle took a few steps, then stopped and turned his head from side to side, as though he was looking for something. "Well, children, this is all very nice, you've all been working very hard, my word haven't you just but who's, I mean, if you follow me, where's your teacher?"

"Tunisia," said Dawn carefully. It was quite a mouthful.

The Professor put his head on one side and screwed up his face in a puzzled way.

"It's a country," explained John helpfully. "She's on holiday in Tunisia . . . He's HOPELESS," he whispered to Jason. "Professors are meant to KNOW."

"But in that case . . ." He fiddled with the buttons on his cardigan. "Who's in charge, if you take my point?"

"Us," said Jason.

The Professor made a noise like a plug being pulled out. Tracy decided he needed looking after and sat him down by the table of exhibits and got him a glass of coke. He kept passing the glass from one hand to the other, as though he didn't know what to do with it. He had heavy hair that flopped forwards over his face, like a spaniel's ears.

"I expect you want to know a bit about the museum," said Tracy, when the silence started to feel uncomfortable. "We've been open two weeks now, and we've had visitors from all over the place."

"We're pretty famous really," said John casually. "We've been on telly twice."

"And we've made pots of money — six and a half marmalade pots," added Rakesh.

Everyone groaned, except the Professor, who seemed to have missed the joke. He was sitting quite still, staring at something as though hypnotized. Then he got up suddenly, poured the coke into the vase of plastic daffodils, and headed for Rakesh's dogs' teeth. He picked them up delicately between finger and thumb and held them at arms' length, then close up under his nose, and peered at them through his spectacles. All the time he hummed a happy little tune to himself.

The children started to feel bored. John tapped his feet and cleared his throat a few times. The Professor didn't notice. He cradled the dogs' teeth in his hand and stroked them with one finger. His lips were curved in a happy smile.

"Would you like a look at Aristotle then?" said Tracy.

The Professor jumped. "So sorry, what was that?"

"Would you like to see Aristotle?" Professor Baffle stared.

"You came here to see our dinosaur," added John patiently.

The Professor's face relaxed. "Of course, I remember now," he said, slipping the dogs' teeth into his trouser pocket.

"Hey," said Rakesh.

The Professor realized what he had done and blushed. "So sorry," he said, and put them back on the table and smiled anxiously at Rakesh.

Tracy led the way to the dinosaur's cage. Aristotle was still flinging himself around in a frenzied dance. The Professor stood with his nose pressed to the chickenwire. "Fascinating. Absolutely fascinating," he kept muttering. "Pterosaurus to a T."

"I don't think he can spell," whispered Jason to Rakesh. Rakesh trod on his foot.

"Well, what d'you think of him?" said John. "We reckon he's a

pterosaurus of the Cretaceous type —
though there are some remains in
the Northern hemisphere that date
from the Jurassic."

"Of course, of course," said the
Professor, taken aback. "Precisely as
described in my book, *Some Fossils of
the Cretaceous Period*."

"Look at Aristotle," whispered
Dawn to Tania, staring at the
dinosaur's furious dance. "I don't
think he liked that bit about fossils."

"D'you want to get in and have a
proper look at him?" asked Tracy.

"It's really very kind of you," said
the Professor, turning to Tracy. The
chickenwire had left a diamond
pattern on his nose. "Very kind
indeed. But I'm not too sure, if you
follow me . . ."

"Go on, we don't mind a bit," said Tania.

"You can't see him properly from here," said John. "If you get in the cage you can get a good look at his teeth."

Still the Professor hesitated. "I . . . I don't suppose it's aggressive at all?" he asked casually.

The children looked at each other. Nobody seemed to know.

"Um, well, we're not too sure," said Rakesh, playing for time. John rushed off to look up "aggressive" in *Burton's Guide to Knowledge*.

"Oh, I know what you mean," said Tracy suddenly. "You mean, does he bite? Don't worry, our Mr Sludge wouldn't hurt a fly."

"Not likely," said Tania, shocked

127

at the suggestion.

"You never can tell with dinosaurs," said Mr Tompsett darkly.

The Professor pushed his hair back from his face and cleared his throat and opened the door of the cage. Then, humming *The Teddy Bears' Picnic* under his breath, he went into the cage.

Aristotle paused in his dance, and shuffled up to the Professor.

"Good doggie, good doggie," said Professor Baffle, as the dinosaur nuzzled his ankle.

"I don't think he's used to animals," whispered Jason to John, who had given up his search in *Burton's Guide to Knowledge*. "Aggressive" turned out to have been in the bit that Aristotle had eaten.

The Professor bent down and patted the dinosaur on the head. "Now, little chap, let's have a good look at those toothipegs of yours. Open up for me, there's a good little chap."

Aristotle thumped his tail on the floor and kept his mouth firmly shut.

"I don't think he likes being talked to like that," said Dawn to Tania.

"Let's just see what we can find," said the Professor. He fumbled in his pocket and pulled out a handful of cabbage leaves. They were slimy at the edges, with a strong mouldy smell. Aristotle retreated to the back of the cage, still thumping his tail fast and fiercely on the floor. His teeth gleamed.

The Professor held out the cabbage leaves towards him. "Here's a nice little dinner for a dinosaur. Come along now, let's have a look at those little tee . . . Aaee! . . .!"

There was a snap of jaws and a cry and a tearing sound, and the Professor came leaping out of the cage with a bit of his trouser leg hanging loose.

Tracy shrieked and all the seaside postcards fell off the wall. "He's bitten him!"

"How could he?"

"Our Mr Sludge!"

The children stared as the Professor collapsed in a chair, making a spluttering noise like a kettle boiling over, clutching his injured leg.

"Mr Tompsett, what shall we . . .?"

But Mr Tompsett was nowhere to be seen.

Tracy went to try and comfort the Professor. She patted his arm. "We're ever so sorry it happened," she said. "But Aristotle hates cabbage. You should have brought him some chocolate."

"Chocolate?" spluttered the Professor. "You feed him on chocolate? But in Chapter 27 of my book it says . . ." He tailed off and stared miserably at his leg. Where the flap of his trouser hung loose, you could see two neat rows of toothmarks and a little trickle of blood the colour of strawberry juice.

"We'd better bandage him up," said Rakesh.

"But what can we bandage him with?"

"It's a Problem," said Dawn.

"There's your T-shirt," said Jason. "It's red, the blood wouldn't show." He pounced on Dawn. She retreated behind the hot-water urn.

Just at that moment, Mr Tompsett appeared from the stock-cupboard.

He had a bag of collage materials in one hand, and his bottle of whisky in the other. He dumped the things down on one of the desks.

"Whisky's just the job in emergencies, so I've heard," said Mr Tompsett.

So Tracy poured a little whisky on her handkerchief, which was very nearly clean. The Professor wriggled away when she put out her hand, but he wasn't quite quick enough. She dabbed her handkerchief on the wound, and the Professor's leg jerked and he made a noise like a fire-engine siren. So Rakesh poured a bit more whisky into a cup and gave it to him to drink. Professor Baffle drank it in one gulp, and sighed heavily.

John scrabbled around in the bag
of materials. There were plenty of
patterns to choose from: pink roses,
green spots, scarlet check. Pausing
only to stuff some wool for his
hamster cage into his pocket, he
chose a design of yellow cabbages on
a purple background. Tania tore the
material into strips. She knew about
first aid: her little sisters were always
grazing their knees.

The Professor watched her
miserably and fiddled with his
cardigan buttons. Even John felt
rather sorry for him. "Just think, sir,
how famous you'll be," he said, to
cheer him up.

"D'you think so?" said the
Professor, looking rather pleased
and going pink.

"No doubt about it," said John. "You know about dinosaurs from the inside now."

"It's very kind of you to say so," said the Professor. "Very kind indeed." He pushed his floppy hair back from his face, and started to hum *Waltzing Matilda* under his breath, a little out of tune.

Tania finished off the Professor's leg with a piece of silver tinsel left over from Christmas and stood back to admire her handiwork. The total effect was very attractive. It seemed a shame to cover it up with the Professorial trouser-leg.

"Now would you like another look at Aristotle before you go?" said Rakesh politely.

The Professor twitched slightly.

He looked around the room rather desperately. "Er . . . I've just remembered," he said. "I've got a meeting in Glasgow in half an hour."

"What a pity!"

"Come back any time," said Tracy.

The Professor twitched again, and made for the door. They watched from the doorway as he dashed out on to the playing field and into the helicopter.

The cause of all the trouble was meanwhile perched on the windowsill, staring out at the helicopter. As the rotor blades started to turn, he jumped up and down on the windowsill, waving the flaps of leathery skin where his front legs had been. And when the helicopter finally took to the air, he

wailed a wild little wail, and stared
after it till it was out of sight, as
though he wanted to join it among
the clouds.

Chapter Nine

Aristotle Sludge's Big Day

"I don't understand it at all," said Tania, after the Professor had gone. "Why should he do a thing like that?"

"It wasn't even a juicy leg," said Rakesh. "All skin and bone! Yuk!"

"I never thought he'd really bite,"

said Tracy. "Not even a hopeless old Professor. I suppose he's growing up," she added sadly.

"Of course he's growing up!" said John. "But why should he start taking bites out of people?"

"It's a Problem," said Dawn. She sat and thought for a moment. "I don't think he's very happy," she said.

For once everyone heard her.

"Happy? Of course he's happy!" said Jason. "Dozing half the day and scoffing all that chocolate!"

"Dawn's right," said Tracy. "Half the time he just sits on the windowsill and watches the seagulls. Like he wants something he can't have."

"Well, there's only one thing for it," said John. He took some chalk and wrote on the blackboard below the Spanish shawl.

"ATTENTION: the Sludge Committee. Meeting today at 11.45 sharp."

"Why not at lunchtime?" said Jason, who wasn't too sure when 11.45 was.

"Think, stupid!"

"Of course, it's Spaghetti Streak," said Rakesh excitedly. "She's going over at 12 o'clock."

"Should make an awful row," said Tracy hopefully.

"Right," said John. "So we'd better get the meeting over by then."

At 11.45 prompt the Sludge Committee met on, at and under the table that had been Miss Purgletwitch's. As it was such an important meeting, they'd decided to invite Mr Tompsett as well. They sat him down in Miss Purgletwitch's chair. But it seemed he wasn't used to Committee meetings. Or perhaps he was quite worn out by the morning's excitement. Whatever the reason, he kept on yawning and closing his eyes.

"Right then," said John. "So let's have a vote on it. Hands up who thinks we'd better do something?"

Everyone's hand went up except Mr Tompsett's.

"Hey, Mr Tompsett, what d'you think?" But Mr Tompsett's eyes were closed. John poked him. "Hey, Mr Tompsett, wake up, we haven't got much time."

"Time?" said Mr Tompsett,

opening one eye. "There's a time for everything, so I've heard tell. A time for finding and a time for losing, a time for doing and a time for dreaming . . ." His head dropped on to his chest.

How could he? thought Tracy crossly. Just when we really need him.

"Motion carried," said John importantly. "So we all think we'd better do something."

"Do what?" said Tracy. There was silence. The children sat and thought, all screwed up like you are when you're thinking. Dawn wrapped herself round a table-leg and Jason hugged the waste-paper basket tightly and Tania got all mixed up in the Spanish shawl.

"I s'pose we could send him to the zoo," said Rakesh.

The girls jumped on him.

"We can't do that! He's ours!"

"Alright, alright, I was only thinking," said Rakesh. "Nothing to get all steamed up about."

"Don't know," said John. "P'raps Rakesh is right. P'raps that's what we ought to do."

"We can't!"

"He's ours, he belongs to us!"

Mr Tompsett opened one eye. "Does he?"

"Of course he's ours!"

"He hatched on OUR Nature Table!"

"We fed him on OUR Mars Bars!"

"We found him in OUR yoghurt carton!"

"Ah, you never can tell with dinosaurs," said Mr Tompsett, and went to sleep again.

"You girls, you're the limit," said Rakesh. "I get an idea, and you jump down my throat!"

"Who jumped down your throat?" said Tania menacingly.

"You did! It's always the same! On and on and . . ."

"Look who's talking! You just watch it, old smelly socks!"

"Watch it yourself. You girls, you're a load of . . ."

"Flying fishsticks!" yelped Tracy, and dived under the desk. With a scream and shriek of engines, and a crashing like thunder that tore the air apart, Spaghetti Streak went over. Everyone scrambled for cover.

All the postcards fell off the wall, and the dead frog leapt a good metre in the air. Rakesh stuffed the plastic daffodils in his ears.

As the sound faded away, leaving a white-hot buzzing in the ears, Jason poked his head out of the wastepaper basket. And he stared in open-mouthed horror at what he saw.

"The wall! Look at the wall!"

For there was a crack in the wall of the Quiet Room, a crack that yawned even wider in the seconds that seemed like hours. And as he watched, the wall bulged out like a sail in the wind.

"Look out!" he shrieked, but no one heard him. For then there was noise all about them: the crashing and clattering of bricks, the snickering of broken glass, a mighty explosion that echoed in their ears like the end of everything.

Then suddenly there was silence. The children stared out from under the table, peered through the dust that smoked up from the crumbled remains of everything, and felt themselves to make sure there were no bits missing.

The cry was loud in the silence. It was a cry of triumph, a glorious wail as wild as stormwinds. Tracy was the first to know. She fought her way through the smoking remains of the room, to the hole in the wall that had once been a window. She peered up, up, into the sky — just in time to see him, wild wings vanishing into the

blue brightness. Aristotle Sludge's
Day had come.

"I can't do lions," said John crossly. "I never know how their noses go."

"Easy peasy. They're all squashed in like Jason's," said Rakesh helpfully. Jason kicked him under the table.

It was lessons as normal for Class 1C. Workmen had moved into their old classroom, and would probably be there for some time, for the supersonic blast had not only brought down the inner wall, and broken all the windows: it had also made a great gash in the outside wall, the hole through which Aristotle Sludge had made his flight to freedom, carried upwards on the air-current trailed by the giant jet. The children had been hopeful that the repairs might postpone things for a bit. But to their disgust, the desks had all been put into a Portakabin, and Miss Purgletwitch was back from Tunisia, looking very brown. She'd just started them off on their next project, which was all about the Romans. There was lots to learn about gladiators and lions and men with nets.

Tracy leaned over to look at John's drawing. She giggled to herself.

"That doughnut you've drawn — why's it got a tail?"

Everyone laughed except John. He threw his pen down in disgust.

"Oh, I give up," he said. "I'm going to make a model." And he went off to the paint cupboard in search of cardboard boxes.

It was as he was sorting out cartons

that he heard it. A mewing, whining, whimpering sound that came from the darkness right at the back of the cupboard. It didn't sound quite like a cat, thought John – the sound was too deep for a cat. He listened as the poor little thing went whimpering on, like a baby. And then came a scuffling scrabbling sound, as of small velvety paws among cereal packets.

John thought about it for a moment. Then he spoke firmly to himself.

"I must be making it up," he said.

He shut the door and went back to his desk.

HIPPO BESTSELLERS

HIPPO BOOKS FOR YOUNGER READERS

If you've enjoyed this book, you'll probably be interested to know that there are loads more Hippo books to suit all kinds of tastes. You'll find scary spooky books, gripping adventure stories, funny books, and lots lots more.

You'll find these and many more fun Hippo books at your local bookshop, or you can order them direct. Just send off to *Customer Services, Hippo Books, Westfield Road, Southam, Leamington Spa, Warwickshire CV33 OJH*, not forgetting to enclose a cheque or postal order for the price of the book(s) plus 30p per book for postage and packing.

We've got lots of great books for younger readers in Hippo's STREAMERS series:

Broomstick Services by Ann Jungman   £1.75
When Joe, Lucy and Jackie find two witches sleeping in the school caretaker's shed, they can't believe their eyes. When they hear that the witches want to be ordinary, they can't believe their ears. But they help the witches set up *Broomstick Services* and then the fun really begins . . .

Paws – A Panda Full of Surprises
by Joan Stimson   £1.75
Every year Uncle Cyril sends Trevor an exciting birthday present. But this year he seems to have forgotten. That is until a smart delivery truck arrives outside Trevor's house bringing the most fantastic present Trevor could ever have dreamed of – Paws!

Aristotle Sludge by Margaret Leroy   £1.75
Class 1C's routing changes completely when Aristotle Sludge explodes into their lives. Looking after a baby dinosaur means a lot of hard work – but with Aristotle Sludge around there's a lot of fun too!

The Old Woman Who Lived In A Roundabout
by Ruth Silvestre   £1.75
When Joe discovers a roundabout whilst out exploring, he can hardly believe his eyes. And when he finds out that an old woman lives in it, he is truly amazed. But, before long Joe and Granny Peg become firm friends and magical things begin to happen . . .

Look out for these other titles in the STREAMERS series:

Nate the Great by Marjorie Sharmat
Nate the Great and the Missing Key by Marjorie Sharmat
Sally Ann – On Her Own by Terrance Dicks
Sally Ann – The School Play by Terrance Dicks
Sally Ann – The Picnic by Terrance Dicks
Sally Ann – Goes to Hospital by Terrance Dicks
The Little Yellow Taxi and His Friends by Ruth Ainsworth